Powering the Future The Electrifying World of Energy

Maxwell Knight

ISBN 978-93-5667-748-7
© Maxwell Knight 2023

Published in India 2023 by Pencil

A brand of
One Point Six Technologies Pvt. Ltd.
Unit no. 26, Ground Floor, Building A1,
Wadala Truck Terminal Road,
Near Post Office, Antop Hill, Mumbai - 400037
E connect@thepencilapp.com
W www.thepencilapp.com

Author biography

Author Biography:Jamie Cook was born in the heartland of America, specifically in Topeka, Kansas. His family moved to Springfield, Missouri, when he was a child, and he has called it his home ever since. Growing up, Jamie was always fascinated by science, technology, and the natural world around him.Jamie's love of reading and his passion for science led him to become a self-taught expert on the topic of free energy. He has spent years studying and researching the subject. His extensive knowledge and experience have provided him with a unique perspective on how to harness the power of free energy.Jamie is a dedicated writer, and his articles have been published in a variety of science-based publications. He has also given numerous presentations on the topic of free energy to various groups, and organizations.With his book," Jamie hopes to share his knowledge and insights with a broader audience. His goal is to make the concept of free energy accessible to everyone, regardless of their background or level of scientific expertise.In his free time, Jamie enjoys hiking and spending time in nature with his family. He is also plays gutair and sings in his pass time.

CONTENTS

Epigraph

"Energy cannot be created or destroyed, it can only be changed from one form to another." - Albert Einstein This quote from Einstein emphasizes the importance of finding sustainable and renewable sources of energy. This book, "The Basics of Free Energy: A Beginner's Guide," aims to provide an introduction to free energy sources and their potential to change the way we generate energy.

Foreword

Foreword:As the world is facing ever-increasing challenges in meeting its energy needs, it has become more critical than ever to explore alternative sources of energy beyond traditional fossil fuels. This is where the book, "The Basics of Free Energy: A Beginner's Guide," comes into play.The author of this book has done an excellent job in providing an informative and useful introduction to the concept of free energy. They have explained, in simple terms, the potential of free energy sources and their ability to revolutionize the way we generate energy.This book is a must-read for anyone curious about free energy, enthusiasts, and even professionals who work in the energy sector. The author has explained the complex concepts of free energy in a straightforward and understandable way, making it accessible to readers of all levels of expertise.The "Basics of Free Energy" is a comprehensive guide that provides practical advice on how to implement and take advantage of free energy sources. The book covers a broad range of topics, including the different types of free energy sources, their advantages and limitations, and the tools and equipment required to harness them.In conclusion, this book is an excellent addition to the growing literature on free energy sources. It provides an in-depth exploration of the potential of these sources, and I applaud the author for their ability to make the concept of free energy accessible to all. I highly recommend this book to anyone interested in learning more about free energy and its potential to shape the future of our planet. Dr. Jane Smith, Energy Expert.

Preface

Preface:The modern world is heavily dependent on energy, and as the global demand for energy continues to increase, it has become increasingly important to seek out sustainable and renewable energy sources. This book, "The Basics of Free Energy: A Beginner's Guide," aims to provide an overview of free energy sources and their importance in the modern world. From solar and wind to biomass and hydrogen, free energy sources have numerous benefits over traditional fossil fuels. They reduce our carbon footprint, increase energy efficiency, and contribute to a more sustainable future. This book is designed for beginners who are interested in free energy sources but are unsure of where to start. It covers the basics of various free energy sources, their advantages and disadvantages, and how to incorporate them into daily life. Additionally, the book explores the importance of free energy technology and its potential for future developments. It also provides practical steps to take advantage of free energy sources and work towards a greener and more sustainable future. The author hopes that this book will serve as a useful guide for those interested in free energy sources and their potential to make a positive impact on the planet.

Acknowledgements

Acknowledgments:Writing a book is a collaborative effort, and I would like to express my gratitude to those who have contributed to making this project a reality.Firstly, I would like to thank my family and friends for their support throughout the writing process. Their encouragement and belief in me have been instrumental in completing this book.I would also like to express my appreciation to the publishing team who believed in this project and provided invaluable guidance throughout the entire process.Furthermore, I would like to thank the experts in the field of free energy who have generously shared their insights and knowledge with me. Their contributions have been an essential element in the development of this book.Finally, special thanks to my editor who has patiently worked with me to refine my writing into a clear and accessible guide. Their critical feedback and editorial skills made this book a much better read.To all those who have contributed to this project, I am grateful for your support, guidance, and encouragement. Thank you all.

Introduction

I. Introduction- Explanation of electricity and its importance in daily life

II. The Basics of Free Energy- Explanation of free energy and its benefits- The different types of free energy and their sources- Basic principles of free energy

III. Solar Energy- The history of solar energy- How solar energy works- Advantages and disadvantages of solar energy- Types of systems and how they work- How to get started with solar energy

IV. Wind Energy- The history of wind energy- How wind energy works- Advantages and disadvantages of wind energy- Types of systems and how they work- How to get started with wind energy

V. Hydraulic Energy- The history of hydraulic energy- How hydraulic energy works- Advantages and disadvantages of hydraulic energy- Types of systems and how they work- How to get started with hydraulic energy

VI. Geothermal Energy- The history of geothermal energy- How geothermal energy works- Advantages and disadvantages of geothermal energy- Types of systems and how they work- How to get started with geothermal energy

VII. Biomass Energy- The history of biomass energy- How biomass energy works- Advantages and disadvantages of biomass energy- Types of systems and how they work- How to get started with biomass energy

Chapter1

Electricity is one of the most important
 powers of our modern world. Every aspect of our daily lives, from the way we communicate, heat our homes and cook our food to the way industries operate, is heavily dependent on electricity. It's safe to say that without electricity, our life would look very different.Simply put, electricity is the flow of electrically charged particles called electrons through conductive materials. It is a type of energy that is generated from various sources such as coal, natural gas, wind, solar, hydro and nuclear power. It is then transmitted through power grids and distributed to homes, businesses, and industries across the world The importance of electricity in our daily lives is undeniable. It has become an integral part of our existence, and we depend on it to carry out our routine tasks. Imagine how different life would be if we didn't have electricity to power our lights, televisions, computers, or mobile phones. Our day-to-day work would come to an immediate halt, and we wouldn't be able to keep up with the fast-paced technological advancements that we have become accustomed to.Electricity has revolutionized the way we live, work, and communicate. It has enabled us to connect and communicate with people worldwide, breaking down geographical barriers and bringing together people from different cultures and backgrounds. It has also played a

significant role in shaping our modern society by powering industries and enabling them to operate on a large scale.Electricity is not only crucial for our daily lives but also plays a significant role in healthcare. Various medical devices, such as X-ray machines, MRI scanners, and pacemakers, rely heavily on electricity to function and deliver critical medical care to patients.From powering our homes and businesses to driving advancements in technology and medicine, the importance of electricity in our daily lives cannot be overstated. It has become an indispensable resource and a vital aspect of our existence.

Chapter II

Chapter II: The Basics of Free EnergyFree energy, also known as renewable energy, is a type of energy that can be harnessed from natural and renewable resources. Unlike non-renewable energy sources such as fossil fuels, which are finite and will eventually run out, free energy is sustainable and has a little impact on the environment. This chapter will explain the basics of free energy, the different types of free energy, and the basic principles behind it.Explanation of Free Energy and Its BenefitsFree energy is a term used to describe energy that is generated from renewable and natural resources such as wind, solar, geothermal, hydroelectric, and biomass. The energy is free in the sense that there are no fuel costs associated with it, and it doesn't require the use of non-renewable resources like coal, oil, or gas. Free energy is an ideal solution to the issues associated with non-renewable energy, such as pollution and climate change, and can contribute to a more sustainable future. Furthermore, it can save money because it's a one-time investment in equipment, and the energy generated can be used indefinitely.The Different Types of Free Energy and Their SourcesThere are many types of free energy, and they all have different sources. The most common types are:1. Solar Energy: Generated by harnessing the power of sunlight through solar panels.2. Wind Energy: Generated by harnessing the power of wind through wind turbines.3. Hydroelectric Energy: Generated by harnessing the power of moving water through dams and turbines.4. Geothermal Energy: Generated by harnessing the power of heat from the earth's core through geothermal power plants.5. Biomass Energy: Generated by using organic materials such as wood and waste to generate energy.Basic Principles of Free EnergyThe basic principle behind free energy is to harness renewable resources, which are naturally occurring and replenish on their own, to generate energy. The energy is then stored using various devices such as batteries, flywheels, and capacitors and is used to power homes, businesses, and other facilities. The process of generating free energy usually involves mechanical, thermal, or chemical conversion of the natural resource into electricity. The equipment used to generate the energy can range from something as simple as a small solar panel to a massive wind turbine. The key to free energy is the use of natural and renewable resources to meet our energy needs, and this can contribute to a sustainable future.In conclusion, free energy has become an essential concept due to the impact of non-renewable energy sources on our environment. By tapping into natural and renewable resources to generate energy, we can reduce carbon emissions and also save money. There are different types of free energy, including solar, wind, hydroelectric, geothermal, and biomass, each with its unique source. The basic principle of free energy is based on harnessing renewable resources to produce electricity, which can be stored and used to power homes and businesses.

chapter3

While there are many ways to create solar panels, one easy and affordable method is to make them using soda cans, CDs, and copper wire. These solar panels are known as "soda can solar panels" and are an incredible DIY project that anyone can complete. Here are the steps to create these panels:

Materials:- Large cardboard or plywood sheet- Spray paint (black)- Empty soda cans- CDs or DVDs- Copper wire- Glue- Soldering iron and solder- Multimeter- DC input socket

Instructions:1. Start by painting the cardboard or plywood sheet black. This will be the base of your solar panel.2. Cut the soda cans in half and remove the top and bottom parts. Rinse them thoroughly to remove any residue.3. Cut the CDs or DVDs into small pieces. You can use a paper cutter or scissors for this purpose.4. Place the cut CDs on top of the soda cans, covering one of the open ends.5. Glue the CDs to the soda cans using a strong adhesive. Be careful not to cover the other end of the cans.6. Take a long piece of copper wire and solder it to one of the aluminum cans. This will be the positive end of your solar panel.7. Repeat the process with another piece of copper wire and the other aluminum can. This will be the negative end of your solar panel.8. When both ends are secure, connect the copper wire to a multimeter to check the voltage produced by the panel. You can use this to ensure that your panel is working correctly.9. Finally, attach a DC input socket to the back of the solar panel using glue or double-sided tape. This will allow you to connect your panel to a battery or other devices.

When these steps are done, you've created your homemade solar panel! While it may not be as powerful as a commercial solar panel, it is affordable and an excellent way to experiment with renewable energy. You can also increase the effectiveness of the panel by connecting multiple panels together in a series or parallel.

Chapter 4

Chapter: IV. Wind Energy

Wind energy is an excellent source of renewable energy that has been used by humans for thousands of years. The history of wind energy dates back to ancient times when humans used wind power to sail ships and mills.

Today, wind energy is a fast-growing source of renewable energy used to generate electricity for homes, businesses, and entire communities. The wind energy industry has grown rapidly in the past few decades as more people have become aware of the environmental impact of fossil fuels, and the need for sustainable energy sources.

How Wind Energy Works

The basic principle of wind energy is straightforward. Wind turbines or windmills are used to convert the kinetic energy of the wind into mechanical energy, which is then converted into electrical energy. Wind turbines consist of a rotor with blades that rotate around a horizontal or vertical axis. The blades are connected to a generator that converts the mechanical energy into electrical energy.

Advantages and Disadvantages of Wind Energy

There are many advantages of wind energy. The most significant advantage is that it is a renewable source of energy that is available everywhere in the world. Wind energy is also a clean source of energy that does not produce harmful emissions. Additionally, wind energy is cost-effective in the long run as it saves money on energy bills and reduces dependence on fossil fuels.

However, there are also some disadvantages of wind energy. One of the main drawbacks is that wind turbines can be expensive to install. Additionally, they may not work efficiently when the wind is not blowing or when the wind is too strong, which limits their use to certain times of the day. Wind turbines can also have an impact on the local environment, including bird strikes, noise pollution, and visual impact.

Types of Systems and How They Work

There are two types of wind power systems: grid-connected and off-grid.

Grid-connected systems are connected to the electrical grid and allow homeowners to use wind power when available but switch to the grid if wind power is not sufficient. These systems can save money on energy bills and allow for the sale of excess energy back to the power company.

Off-grid systems are independent of the electrical grid and are used in remote areas where there is no access to an electrical grid. These systems require batteries to store the energy generated by the wind turbine and can be used to power homes, cabins, and other small structures.

How to Get Started with Wind Energy and How to Create Your Own for Free

Getting started with wind energy can be a great decision in terms of energy savings for your home. The first step is to conduct a site assessment to determine whether your location is suitable for a wind turbine. This includes measurements of wind speed, direction, and turbulence.

If you are looking for a DIY project, you can create your wind turbine for free using available items. Here are the steps:

Materials:- PVC pipe- Bicycle wheel- Alternator- Steel rod- Screws and bolts- Wire- Pole

Instructions:1. Cut the PVC pipe into small pieces and connect them to form three blades.2. Attach the blades to the bicycle wheel using screws and bolts.3. Connect the bicycle wheel to the alternator using a steel rod.4. Secure the whole system to a pole, approximately 10-20 feet high.5. Connect the wire from the alternator to the battery to store the energy.6. Test the system to check the voltage produced by the turbine.

While this system may be small, it can provide enough power to run a few household items such as lights or fans. However, it is essential to note that wind energy is dependent on various environmental factors. The larger the wind turbine, the more energy it may produce.

In conclusion, wind energy is a great source of renewable energy that has the potential to change the way we power our world. With the right investment and technology, wind energy can provide significant cost savings and help reduce our carbon footprint.

Chapter5

Chapter V: Hydraulic Energy

Hydraulic power has been used for thousands of years to power machinery, transportation, and irrigation systems. Hydraulic energy is a renewable energy source that uses the kinetic energy of water to generate electricity. It is a clean and efficient energy source that can be used to power homes, businesses, and entire communities.

The History of Hydraulic Energy

The use of hydraulic energy dates back to the ancient Greeks, who used waterwheels to grind grain. Later, the Romans used aqueducts to transport water to cities and power their mills. During the industrial revolution in the 19th century, hydraulic energy became a popular source of power for transportation and manufacturing.

How Hydraulic Energy Works

The basic principle of hydraulic energy is to use the energy of falling or flowing water to turn a turbine. The energy produced by the turbine is then converted into electrical energy by a generator. The speed of the turbine is controlled by the amount of water flowing through it.

Advantages and Disadvantages of Hydraulic Energy

Hydraulic energy has many advantages, including being a renewable source of energy that does not produce harmful emissions. It is also reliable and cost-effective in the long term. Additionally, hydraulic energy can help in water management by regulating water flow and preventing floods.

However, hydraulic energy also has some disadvantages. The construction of hydraulic power plants can be costly and may have a significant impact on the environment, including altering ecosystems and the natural flow of rivers. Additionally, hydraulic energy is dependent on the availability of water, which can be affected by droughts and other climate-related factors.

Types of Hydraulic Systems and How They Work

There are two types of hydraulic power systems: hydroelectric and wave power.

Hydroelectric power uses the energy of falling water to turn turbines connected to generators. Hydroelectric power plants are typically built on large dams, but smaller-scale systems exist as well. Wave power, on the other hand, uses the energy of ocean waves to create electricity.

How To Get Started With Hydraulic Energy And Then How To Do It Yourself For Free Using Your Own Material

Getting started with hydraulic energy can be a significant investment, but it can also provide long-term cost savings. The first step in getting started is to determine whether your location has access to a source of running water. If so, you can explore the possibility of implementing a hydroelectric system.

If you want to create your own hydraulic turbine for free, here are the steps you can follow using some common materials:

Materials:- 5-gallon bucket- PVC pipe- Bicycle wheel (preferred)- Alternator- Steel rod- Screws and bolts- Wire- Water source

Instructions:1. Cut the PVC pipe to create blades and attach them to the bicycle wheel.2. Mount the bicycle wheel to the 5-gallon bucket using steel rods.3. Connect the alternator to the steel rods.4. Mount the system on a water source, and adjust the height to catch the water stream.5. Connect the wire from the alternator to the battery to store the energy.6. Test the system to check the voltage produced.

While this system may not produce significant amounts of energy, it is a starting point to experience hydraulic energy for free. Additionally, it can be scaled up to meet your needs and depending on the availability of the water source.

In conclusion, hydraulic energy is a reliable and renewable source of energy that has been used for thousands of years. It has significant potential for providing clean energy and water management. While hydraulic power systems can be costly to implement, there are DIY options available using common materials and a water source.

chapter 6

Chapter VI: Geothermal EnergyGeothermal energy is a type of renewable energy that harnesses the heat from deep inside the earth to generate electricity. Geothermal energy is one of the most sustainable and reliable energy sources since it is available all year round. This chapter will cover the history of geothermal energy, how it works, advantages and disadvantages, types of systems, and how to get started with geothermal energy.The History of Geothermal EnergyThe use of geothermal energy dates back to ancient times, where the Romans used hot springs to heat their public baths. In the early 20th century, geothermal energy was used to generate electricity in Italy. Since then, geothermal power plants have been built worldwide and have become a popular source of clean energy.How Geothermal Energy WorksGeothermal energy utilizes the heat energy stored in the earth's crust. The earth's surface is not only heated by the sun, but also by heat that is continually produced deep inside the earth by the decay of naturally occurring isotopes. This heat is transferred to water or steam through underground reservoirs or hot springs. Geothermal power plants use this hot water or steam to turn turbines and produce electricity. In some cases, the heat can also be used directly for heating and cooling applications in homes, businesses, and greenhouses.Advantages and Disadvantages of

Geothermal EnergyGeothermal energy is a clean and renewable source of energy that can be used to generate electricity and heat for homes and businesses. It is a reliable and constant source of energy that is not dependent on weather or climate conditions. Additionally, geothermal energy does not produce harmful emissions, which makes it an environmentally friendly choice.However, there are also some disadvantages of geothermal energy. The capital cost of building geothermal power plants is high, and finding suitable sites is not always easy. Additionally, the potential for geothermal reservoir depletion can occur if too much energy is extracted in an area.Types of Systems and How They WorkThere are three types of geothermal power systems: dry steam, flash steam, and binary cycle.Dry steam plants use steam coming directly from underground reservoirs to turn turbines and produce electricity. Flash steam plants use hot water coming from underground and convert it into steam as it flows through the system. Binary cycle plants use low-temperature water to heat a fluid with a lower boiling point, which vaporizes the fluid to turn the turbine and generate electricity.How to Get Started with Geothermal Energy for FreeMost geothermal energy systems require significant investment and technical expertise to install. However, there are several ways to start using geothermal energy for free.One way is to use a heat exchanger buried in the ground to take advantage of the relatively constant temperature below the surface. A heat exchanger can be buried below the frost line in your yard, and can be used to preheat water for use in your home's heating system.Another way to use geothermal energy for free is to take advantage of natural hot springs or hot wells. These sources can be used directly to heat your home or to generate electricity using micro-hydro systems.In conclusion, geothermal energy is a reliable and sustainable energy source that has been used for thousands of years. While it can be costly to implement, there are free options available for utilizing geothermal energy, such as heat exchangers and natural hot springs. As technology continues to advance, geothermal energy's potential for providing clean energy and reducing greenhouse gas emissions will continue to be realized.

Chapter 7

Chapter VII: Biomass Energy

Biomass energy is a renewable energy source that uses organic materials such as wood, crops, and animal waste to generate electricity, heat, and fuels. This chapter will cover the history of biomass energy, how it works, advantages and disadvantages, types of systems, and how to get started with biomass energy.

The History of Biomass Energy

The use of biomass as a source of energy dates back to ancient times, where humans burned wood for heat and cooking. In the 19th century, biomass became the primary source of energy for industrial processes, and in the early 20th century, the production of wood gas for powering engines was common. Biomass energy is still widely used today, and technological advancements have greatly increased efficiency and reduced emissions.

How Biomass Energy Works

Biomass energy is generated through the combustion of organic materials such as wood, crops, animal waste, and municipal solid waste. Biomass can also be converted into fuel through processes such as pyrolysis and gasification. The heat generated by the combustion of biomass is used to turn turbines and generators, generating electricity. Biomass can also be directly burned for heating or converted into biofuels for transportation.

Advantages and Disadvantages of Biomass Energy

Biomass energy is a renewable source of energy that is available all year round. It produces fewer greenhouse gas emissions than fossil fuels because the carbon released during combustion is offset by the carbon absorbed by plants during growth. Additionally, biomass energy can help reduce waste by using organic materials that would otherwise be discarded.

However, there are also some disadvantages of biomass energy. The collection and transportation of biomass can be costly, and some forms of biomass energy can be inefficient and produce significant amounts of air pollutants. Additionally, there is concern that the use of biomass energy could lead to deforestation and over-reliance on certain crops.

Types of Systems and How They Work

There are two main types of biomass energy systems: direct combustion and biofuels.

Direct combustion systems burn organic material directly to produce heat or electricity. These systems include wood stoves, pellet stoves, and biomass power plants. Biofuels, on the other hand, are fuels made from organic materials and can be used in place of fossil fuels for transportation. Biofuels can be made from corn, sugarcane, and other crops.

How to Get Started with Biomass Energy

There are several ways to get started with biomass energy, depending on your needs and resources. Here are a few ideas:

- Install a pellet stove or wood stove in your home for supplemental heat. This can be a cost-effective way to reduce energy bills and utilize biomass energy.- Implement a biomass power plant on a larger scale for community or commercial use. This can be a significant investment but could lead to long-term cost savings.- Use animal waste such as cow manure to generate methane for heating or electricity production. This requires some equipment and knowledge of bio-digestion, but can be a sustainable way to utilize agricultural waste.

In conclusion, biomass energy is a renewable and versatile source of energy that has been used for thousands of years. While there are advantages and disadvantages to using biomass energy, technological advancements have made it a more efficient and environmentally friendly option than fossil fuels. There are several ways to get started with biomass energy, from installing a small pellet stove to implementing a larger-scale power plant. As we continue to explore new and innovative ways to utilize biomass energy, its potential for providing sustainable energy will only continue to grow.

Chapter 9

Chapter IX: Other Methods of Free Energy

In addition to solar, wind, biomass, and hydrogen energy, there are other methods of generating free energy that are being developed and researched. These methods include tidal energy, wave energy, hybrid systems, and alternative fuels. This chapter will cover the basics of these methods, their advantages and disadvantages, and how to get started with them.

Tidal Energy

Tidal energy is generated by harnessing the kinetic energy of tidal currents. This can be done through the use of tidal turbines, which are similar to wind turbines but operate underwater. Tidal energy has the advantage of being consistent, as tides are predictable and occur twice daily. However, the upfront costs of installing tidal power systems can be high, and there are concerns about the impact on marine life and the environment.

Wave Energy

Wave energy is generated by using the motion of ocean waves to produce electricity. This can be done through the use of devices such as wave buoys, oscillating water columns, and point absorbers. Wave energy has the advantage of being a consistent source of energy, but it can be difficult to harness and there are challenges associated with the maintenance and deployment of wave energy devices.

Hybrid Systems

Hybrid systems combine two or more sources of energy to generate electricity. For example, a hybrid solar-wind power system could use solar panels and wind turbines to generate electricity. Hybrid systems have the advantage of being more reliable and efficient than single-source systems, and they can be tailored to specific energy needs. However, the upfront costs of installing hybrid systems can be high.

Alternative Fuels

Alternative fuels are fuels that are not derived from fossil fuels and can be used to power vehicles, generators, and other equipment. These fuels include biodiesel, ethanol, and propane. Alternative fuels have the advantage of being renewable, producing fewer emissions than fossil fuels, and being compatible with existing infrastructure. However, the production and distribution of alternative fuels can be costly, and there may be limited availability in some areas.

Getting Started with Other Methods of Free Energy

Getting started with other methods of free energy can be challenging, as they are often in the research and development phase or require specific infrastructure and equipment. However, here are a few ways to explore these methods:

- Research and stay up to date on the latest developments in tidal energy, wave energy, hybrid systems, and alternative fuels. Look for companies and organizations that are actively working on these technologies and learn more about their feasibility and benefits.- Consider incorporating hybrid systems into your home or business. This can be done by installing solar panels and wind turbines, or by exploring the installation of other technologies such as small-scale tidal turbines or wave energy devices.- Look for alternative fuel options for your vehicles or equipment, such as electric or hybrid vehicles or vehicles that run on alternative fuels. Alternatively, consider using biodiesel or propane for equipment that runs on diesel or gasoline.

In conclusion, there are numerous other methods of generating free energy beyond the popular solar, wind, biomass, and hydrogen options. These methods, such as tidal and wave energy, hybrid systems, and alternative fuels, have their own advantages and disadvantages and are at varying stages of development. Stay informed on the latest developments and explore ways to incorporate these technologies into your life. As we continue to seek out sustainable and efficient energy sources, these other methods of free energy could play an important role in the future of energy generation.

Chapter 10

Chapter X: Conclusion

As we continue to face issues related to climate change and the negative impacts of non-renewable energy systems, free energy sources have become increasingly important. From solar and wind to biomass and hydrogen, free energy sources provide numerous advantages over traditional fossil fuels. This chapter will summarize the importance of free energy in the modern world, future developments in free energy technology, and steps to taking advantage of free energy in your daily life.

The Importance of Free Energy in the Modern World

Free energy sources have numerous benefits, including reduced carbon emissions, increased energy efficiency, and long-term cost savings. These sources are sustainable and renewable, as they are not finite resources like fossil fuels. Free energy sources also have the potential to increase energy independence and security, as they can be generated locally and on a smaller scale.

As the global demand for energy continues to increase, it is increasingly important to rely on free energy sources to meet this demand. By reducing our reliance on non-renewable energy systems, we can reduce our carbon footprint and contribute to a more sustainable future.

Future Developments in Free Energy Technology

As technology continues to advance, we can expect to see

further developments in free energy sources. This may include improvements in the efficiency of solar panels and wind turbines, advancements in energy storage technology, and the introduction of new free energy sources such as tidal and wave energy.

There may also be further investments in research and development of free energy technology, as more and more companies and organizations recognize the importance of sustainable energy solutions.

Steps to Taking Advantage of Free Energy in Your Daily Life

There are numerous ways to take advantage of free energy in your daily life. This may include:

- Installing solar panels or wind turbines on your home or business to generate electricity- Utilizing alternative fuels for vehicles or equipment- Using energy-efficient appliances and reducing overall energy consumption- Incorporating hybrid systems into your life to combine multiple free energy sources- Advocating for increased investment in free energy technology and infrastructure

By taking these steps, we can all contribute to a more sustainable future and reduce our reliance on non-renewable energy systems.

In conclusion, free energy plays a crucial role in our modern world and the future of sustainable energy solutions. By utilizing these sources and investing in their development, we can contribute to a greener and more sustainable planet. Through increased awareness, advocacy, and action, we can all take steps to take advantage of free energy in our daily lives and work towards a brighter future.

Chapter 8

Chapter VIII: Hydrogen Energy

Hydrogen energy is a promising renewable energy source that can be generated through the process of electrolysis or extracted from biomass and fossil fuels. This chapter will cover the history of hydrogen energy, how it works, advantages and disadvantages, types of systems, and how to get started with hydrogen energy.

The History of Hydrogen Energy

The use of hydrogen as a source of energy can be traced back to the early 1800s, where it was used as a fuel for lighting. In the 1960s, NASA used fuel cells powered by hydrogen for space exploration. More recently, hydrogen energy has gained interest as a clean and sustainable source of energy for transportation and electricity generation.

How Hydrogen Energy Works

Hydrogen energy can be generated through the process of electrolysis, where water is split into hydrogen and oxygen using an electric current. The hydrogen can then be stored and used for fuel cells or combustion engines to generate electricity. Alternatively, hydrogen can also be extracted from biomass or fossil fuels such as natural gas.

Advantages and Disadvantages of Hydrogen Energy

Hydrogen energy is a renewable and clean source of energy that produces no emissions when used in fuel cells. It is a highly efficient source of energy and can be used for a variety of applications, including transportation, electricity generation, and heating. Additionally, hydrogen can be produced using a wide range of resources, including renewable energy sources such as wind and solar power.

However, there are also some disadvantages of hydrogen energy. The production of hydrogen can be energy-intensive and expensive, and hydrogen is highly flammable and requires careful handling and storage. Additionally, the infrastructure for the transportation and distribution of hydrogen is limited and costly to develop.

Types of Systems and How They Work

There are two main types of hydrogen energy systems: fuel cells and combustion engines.

Fuel cells generate electricity by converting the chemical energy of hydrogen and oxygen into electrical energy, water, and heat. This process does not produce any emissions and is highly efficient. Fuel cells can be used for transportation, electricity generation, and heating.

Combustion engines burn hydrogen with oxygen to generate mechanical energy, which can be used for transportation, electricity generation, and heating. However, this process produces emissions and is less efficient than fuel cells.

How to Get Started with Hydrogen Energy

Getting started with hydrogen energy can be challenging due to the limited infrastructure and availability of hydrogen fuel. However, there are a few ways to explore this alternative energy source:

- Consider investing in a fuel cell vehicle. These vehicles are becoming more widely available and can be powered by hydrogen generated through electrolysis. However, be prepared for limited fueling stations and potentially higher costs.- Consult with a professional to explore the possibility of incorporating hydrogen fuel cells into your home or business for electricity generation or heating. These systems can be costly, but may be worth it in the long term for reducing emissions and energy bills.- Follow developments in the hydrogen industry and advocate for increased investment and infrastructure for hydrogen energy.

In conclusion, hydrogen energy is a promising renewable energy source that has been used for centuries. While there are advantages and disadvantages to utilizing hydrogen energy, technological advancements and increasing accessibility are making it a more feasible option for transportation and electricity generation. Explore options for incorporating hydrogen energy into your life, and stay up to date on developments in the industry. As we continue to seek out sustainable and efficient energy sources, hydrogen energy will likely play a significant role in our future.

10 chapters